MISSI

Flame

Have you seen this kitten?

Flame is a magic kitten of royal blood, missing from his own world.
His uncle, Ebony, is very keen that he is found quickly.
Flame may be hard to spot as he often appears in a
variety of fluffy kitten colours but you can recognize him
by his big emerald eyes and whiskers that crackle with magic!

He is believed to be looking for a young friend to take care of him.

Could it be you?

If you find this very special kitten please let Ebony,
ruler of the Lion Throne, know.

Sue Bentley's books for children often include animals or fairies. She lives in Northampton and enjoys reading, going to the cinema, and sitting watching the frogs and newts in her garden pond. If she hadn't been a writer, she would probably have been a skydiver or brain surgeon. The main reason she writes is that she can drink pots and pots of tea while she's typing. She has met and owned many cats, and each one has brought a special sort of magic to her life.

Magic Kitten

Star Dreams

SUE BENTLEY

Illustrated by Angela Swan

PUFFIN

PUFFIN BOOKS

UK | USA | Canada | Ireland | Australia
India | New Zealand | South Africa

Puffin Books is part of the Penguin Random House group of companies
whose addresses can be found at global.penguinrandomhouse.com.

puffinbooks.com

Penguin
Random House
UK

First published 2006
This edition published 2016
001

Text copyright © Sue Bentley, 2006
Illustrations copyright © Angela Swan, 2006

The moral right of the author and illustrator has been asserted

Set in Bembo 15pt/22pt
Printed in Great Britain by Clays Ltd, St Ives plc

A CIP catalogue record for this book is available from the British Library

ISBN: 978-0-141-36778-1

www.greenpenguin.co.uk

To Bernie – little blue-cream sister

★Prologue★

As a terrifying roar rang out, the
young white lion froze. He should
have known it was too dangerous to
come back home. He needed to act
quickly.

Sparks crackled in Flame's fur and there
was a flash of dazzling white light. Where
he had stood now sat a silky cream kitten
with spotted brown markings.

An old grey lion appeared in the long grass at Flame's side. 'Prince Flame! You shouldn't be here. You must hide!'

'There is no time, Cirrus!' Flame mewed, trembling. 'Uncle Ebony is almost upon us!'

With a paw almost as big as Flame now was himself, Cirrus gently drew the kitten down to hide in the long grass beside him.

The ground shook as an enormous adult lion pushed through the grass. He stopped barely a metre away from the tiny cream kitten and the old lion. Raising his head, he shook his mane and sniffed the air.

Flame's heart beat fast in his little

body. He was sure they would be found.

At last, Ebony seemed satisfied. He began moving away. 'My nephew will never regain the throne. It is mine now. My spies will find him soon!' he rumbled to himself.

Flame waited until Ebony had gone, then scrambled to his feet. His emerald eyes flashed with anger. 'One day I shall rule, Cirrus!'

Cirrus showed his worn teeth in a smile. 'Indeed you will, Prince Flame, but first you must grow strong and powerful. Use your kitten disguise and return now to the other world.'

Silver sparks glittered in Flame's cream and brown fur as the tiny kitten felt the power building inside him. He mewed a sad farewell and felt himself falling. Falling . . .

★Chapter★
ONE

When Jemma Watson saw the new
poster on the school noticeboard, she
felt her heart beat faster.

Have you got what it takes to be a star?
Auditions for places at A-One Stage
School. Town hall. Saturday 6 May.
Everyone welcome.

Jemma did a quick sum in her head. The auditions were the Saturday after next. Today was Thursday, so she had just over a week to get ready.

'Isn't it brilliant! Are you going for it?' asked an excited voice at her shoulder. It was Fran Bradshaw, the newest girl in Jemma's class.

Jemma knew that some of the schoolkids thought Fran was a bit posh. But she hadn't had much chance to get to know her yet. Anyway, she liked to make up her own mind about people.

She turned and smiled at Fran. 'I haven't decided yet. I don't know if I'd be good enough.'

'Me too. It's a bit scary, isn't it?' Fran said, her blue eyes wide.

Jemma grinned. She tossed her long brown hair over her shoulder. 'Scary is a big hairy spider in the bath. Or telling Mr Butler you haven't done your homework!'

Fran laughed. 'You're right. So going for this audition is . . .'

'Terrifying!' Jemma said, rolling her eyes. She shouldered her school bag and went towards the school exit with

Fran. They passed the playing fields and tennis courts as they walked down the drive. Beyond the front gates, Jemma could see lots of cars drawing up ready to pick kids up and take them home.

'I've got an idea,' Fran said. 'Why don't we practise our routines together? You could come round tonight. We can ask my mum. She's coming to pick me up.'

Jemma's spirits sank. She would love to accept Fran's invitation. 'I can't tonight,' she said reluctantly.

'OK.' Fran's pretty face clouded, then she brightened. 'What about tomorrow night? I could come to your house straight after school, if you like.'

'No!' It was out before Jemma could stop herself. 'Sorry. I mean, I'll have to let you know.'

Fran gave her a puzzled look, but she shrugged. 'Fine by me.'

They had reached the school gate and Jemma saw Fran run over to a sleek silver car. It had an open roof and smart leather seats. It looked very expensive.

'Hi, darling,' Mrs Bradshaw called to her daughter. 'Who's your new friend? Would she like a lift home?'

'Thanks, Mrs Bradshaw, but I haven't got far to go,' Jemma called out quickly. 'See you tomorrow, Fran!'

Jemma opened the shabby front door and edged round the pushchair and broken bike blocking the hall. She went into the kitchen.

'Hi, Mum,' she called.

Mrs Watson was cutting up potatoes. 'Hi, love. Good day at school?'

'It was OK,' Jemma replied. She told her mum about the poster as she filled the sink with hot water and started washing the pile of breakfast dishes. 'It's a great chance to get into stage school, isn't it? Can I go in for the auditions?' she asked eagerly.

Mrs Watson smiled. 'I think you should. You've got a lovely voice.'

Jemma went over to give her a hug. 'Thanks, Mum. I might practise with Fran Bradshaw, a new girl in my class. She's really nice.'

Mrs Watson patted her daughter's arm. 'You should be spending more time with your friends, instead of helping at home all the time.'

'I don't mind,' Jemma said, going across to her baby sister, Poppy, who sat in a high chair chewing her toast. Poppy gave Jemma a gummy grin.

'Hello, Cheeky!' Jemma kissed her sister's fluffy blonde head before going to the sink to fill the kettle. 'I'll make us a cup of tea.'

'Lovely! I've just got time for one before I collect the papers.' Mrs Watson did a paper round every night after she got home from her job at the supermarket. Sometimes Jemma helped her deliver the papers.

'Maybe you could ask Fran round sometime?' Mrs Watson suggested.

Jemma glanced through the kitchen window at the tall weeds and blown-down garden fence. A picture of

Fran's mum's smart car filled her mind.

'I might do,' she said, but she knew she wouldn't.

A guilty feeling welled up inside her. Her mum was a single parent and she did the best she could, but Jemma sometimes got fed up of always having to make do.

'Bah, bah!' Poppy said, squashing toast in her chubby hands.

'Same to you!' Jemma bent down so that her face was level with her baby sister's. Poppy was a happy little girl with a sweet round face and big brown eyes.

'I'm going to go to an audition and win a place to stage school. Yes, I am!' Jemma said in a playful voice, so that Poppy gurgled with laughter.

'Oh, yeah! Who says so?' shouted a cheeky voice.

'Hi, Georgie!' Jemma didn't turn round as her brother came crashing through the back door. At eight years old, he was two years younger than Jemma. She heard the clunks as his football boots and then his school bag landed in a heap on the floor.

'I'm starving! What's for tea?' demanded Georgie.

'It's not ready yet.' Jemma straightened up and spun round. 'Oh!'

Georgie stood there, grinning. There was mud all over his school trousers. His white shirt was streaked with grass stains. And as for his face – Jemma could hardly see his freckles for all the mud spatters.

'What?' said Georgie, shrugging his shoulders.

Jemma couldn't understand how boys always get so messy. Put Georgie in a totally empty room and he'd come out looking like he'd been fighting with Fungus the Bogeyman!

Mrs Watson turned round. She shook her head slowly at Georgie. 'Oh, my goodness! What are you like? You'd better get changed and have a bath.'

Georgie plonked himself down at the table. 'Can't now. I'll pass out if I don't eat something.'

Jemma grinned at her brother. 'Milk and biscuits OK?' She opened the fridge and took out the milk container. It was empty. 'I'll have to go to the shop. Keep an eye on Poppy while Mum's cooking,' she told Georgie.

'OK. But there's no way I'm changing her,' Georgie said around a mouthful of biscuit.

Jemma asked her mum for some money, and then set off for Mr Shah's newsagent's. It took her a couple of minutes to walk to the end of the street and cross the road. Mr Shah sold all kinds of food and sweets as well as newspapers and magazines. Jemma got the milk, then used the last of her pocket money to buy a cherry cake that was on special offer. They could all have it for pudding.

As she came out of the shop, something in the side alley caught her eye. She stopped and stared at the wheelie bins and piles of cardboard boxes. There it was again. A bright glow was coming from behind one of the bins.

Jemma frowned. She went into the alley and bent down to look behind the bin. Puzzled, Jemma wondered if it might be some kind of lamp that someone had thrown away before the batteries had run down.

Then the glow started to get

brighter. Whatever it was, was coming towards her!

Jemma almost dropped the milk. Two bright emerald eyes stared at her from the gloom.

There was an angry hissing noise and suddenly Jemma realized what she was staring at.

An enormous white lion crept slowly out from behind the bin and walked towards Jemma, his head held high and tail erect. A fountain of silver sparks fizzed and crackled in the air around him.

Jemma froze in terror, her heart in her mouth. What was a lion doing here? Was he going to attack her?

'I am Prince Flame. Heir to the Lion

Throne,' growled the lion. 'Who are
you?'

'Whoa!' Jemma almost jumped out of
her skin. He could talk!

★ Chapter ★
TWO

Panic clutched at Jemma's chest. She stood there in complete shock as Flame put his head on one side, waiting for an answer.

'I'm . . . er, Jemma. Jemma Watson. I live just round the corner,' she stammered nervously. The amazing white lion's claws and teeth were very long and sharp.

Flame's eyes narrowed as he gave a satisfied smile. 'Ah. You are a friend. Good,' he purred.

There was a dazzling silver flash.

Jemma was blinded for a second. She blinked hard and rubbed her eyes. When she could see again, the lion had gone. In his place was a cute cream and brown kitten.

'What just happened?' Jemma gasped,

feeling some of the fear drain away. But she still felt really weird about talking to a cat. 'Where's . . . Flame?'

'I am Flame,' the kitten mewed. He had a pink nose, tiny paws and fuzzy fur with spotted brown markings.

'But how? Where's . . .? What?' Jemma shook her head in confusion.

She must be dreaming. This was the Kingsley Estate, where she had lived all her life. Where the most exciting thing that happened was the annual car boot sale behind the church rooms. Glowing white lions just did not appear in alleys and then magically turn into cute kittens.

Flame took a wobbly step forward, and stood right in front of Jemma. He blinked up at her with scared, emerald-green eyes. 'I need to hide. Jemma, can you help me?' he mewed urgently.

He looked so sweet and helpless. Leaning down, Jemma gently picked Flame up and cuddled him. The kitten purred softly and his fur sparkled with hundreds of tiny silver lights.

Jemma felt a strange prickly warmth against her palms. She wondered if Flame was going to turn into something else, but nothing more happened. All at once the sparks disappeared and Jemma's hands stopped tingling.

Flame reached up and touched Jemma's face with one tiny paw. 'My enemies are searching for me. If they find me, they will kill me.'

'What enemies? Who's after you?' Jemma asked.

'Uncle Ebony. He rules my kingdom. He has sent spies to take me back,' replied Flame.

Jemma wanted to ask lots more about Flame's world, but someone might come past at any minute and see them.

She made up her mind. 'I'm taking care of you from now on. You're coming home with me.' She zipped her jacket up around Flame. 'Just wait until Georgie sees you!'

Flame stiffened. 'You can tell no one that I am a prince!'

Jemma felt disappointed. Georgie would have loved to know about Flame, but she wasn't going to do anything that put him in danger.

'OK. Don't worry. Your secret's safe,' she said. With the milk and cake in one hand and Flame tucked under her arm, she set off for home.

'I'm sorry, but you know we can't afford pets, Jemma,' Mrs Watson said firmly, ten minutes later. 'We'll phone the RSPCA. They'll find the kitten a good home.'

'But Flame's special, Mum! He chose me to be his owner,' Jemma said. *Oh,*

*no, she hadn't meant to say that! She must
be more careful.*

Luckily her mum just laughed. 'You
and your imagination, Jemma Watson!'

Jemma bit her lip. How could she
change her mum's mind? She just *had*
to let Flame live with them. He was in
danger and only she could keep him
safe. 'Please, Mum. I'll look after him.
He can sleep in my room. And I'll buy
his food from my pocket money and
everything.'

'Slow down, love. You know how
you always rush into things,' her mum
said calmly.

'I know. But this is different,' Jemma
insisted. 'Please, Mum.'

'Oh, go on, Mum,' urged Georgie,
who was rolling a soft ball across the

rug for Poppy to play with. 'I've thought of an ace name for him . . . Fang.'

'I don't think so!' Jemma scoffed. She put on her best pleading voice. 'Can Flame at least stay for tonight? Please?'

Her mum sighed and gave in. 'I suppose he may as well. But you must put a card in the shop window tomorrow. If an owner comes calling, there'll be no arguments.'

'Thanks, Mum!' Jemma almost leapt out of the chair and gave her mum a hug.

'Can I feed Fang?' Georgie asked.

'Flame!' Jemma corrected her little brother again. Then her face fell. 'We haven't got any cat food. What's Flame going to eat?'

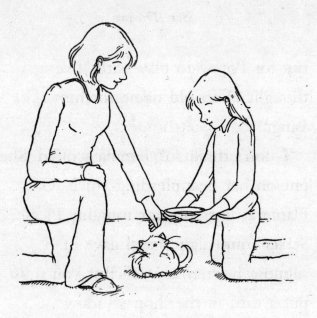

'Give him some milk for now, but too much isn't good for cats,' Mrs Watson said. 'You'd better get some cat food tomorrow, Jemma.'

Jemma bit her lip. She had just remembered spending the last of her pocket money on the cherry cake. How was she going to afford cat food?

Her mum seemed to know what she was thinking. She came over and

pressed a couple of coins into Jemma's
hand. 'That should tide you over until
your next pocket money.'

'Thanks, Mum. You're the best!'
Jemma said, beaming.

'Can I have some money too?'
Georgie piped up hopefully.

'You wish!' Jemma chuckled and
ruffled her brother's sandy hair.

Once Flame had finished his milk,
she took him upstairs. It was cosy in
her bedroom with the evening sun
pouring through the pink curtains. She
scooped the duvet into a nest around
the kitten. 'There, how's that?'

Flame yawned, showing a tiny pink
tongue and sharp white teeth. 'Good. I
am warm now,' he mewed sleepily.
'Jemma, will you keep my secret?'

'Cross my heart and hope to die,' Jemma said. When Flame looked alarmed, she giggled. 'It means I promise not to tell anyone,' she said, stroking his soft ears.

Flame gave her a whiskery grin and tucked his nose into his paws before settling down to sleep.

Jemma sat on her bed beside him. A bubble of happiness rose up from inside her. 'I can't believe this is happening!' she breathed. 'This is so cool!'

The following morning, Jemma woke to the sound of loud purring close to her ear.

Rubbing her eyes, she sat up. It had been late when she went to bed. She'd had to scribble a note about Flame for

Mr Shah's shop window and finish her homework. After that, she'd spent ages trying to decide on a song for the audition.

Flame uncurled himself. He stuck all four paws out and stretched his legs. 'I slept well. I feel safe here,' he mewed.

'You are safe, with me!' Jemma said with a broad smile. She kissed the top of his soft little head.

Just then, the bedroom door flew open and Georgie exploded into the room. He leapt on the bed and began making a fuss of Flame.

'How are you then, Fang?' he asked.

Jemma gave her brother a shove. 'Ow! Get off, you big lump, you're squashing me! And his name's not Fang!'

'Sausage!' Georgie said, using his word for 'sorry'. 'Flame's a rubbish name for a cat.'

'No, it's not . . .' Jemma began. Suddenly she caught sight of her bedside clock. 'Oh, no! We've all overslept!' she groaned, throwing back the duvet. 'Quick, Georgie. Get yourself washed and dressed.'

When Georgie had gone out, Flame

jumped off the bed and padded after Jemma. 'May I help?' he mewed.

'Thanks, Flame, but I'm fine.' Jemma's head was full of all the things she had to do before school. She quickly pulled on her uniform, and then dragged a brush through her hair. Out on the landing she bumped into her mum.

Mrs Watson was still in her dressing gown. Her hair was all on end and she looked worried. 'Oh, dear. I've still got to iron my uniform. I can't be late for work today. We've got staff training.'

'Don't worry, Mum. I'll see to Poppy,' Jemma offered.

'Thanks love,' her mum said with a relieved smile.

As Jemma went to the cot and picked up her baby sister, Flame padded

into the room after her. He wrinkled
his nose and screwed up his face. 'What
is that bad smell?'

'It's just Poppy's nappy,' Jemma said
with a chuckle. 'Come on, stinky little
sis. You *really* need a bath!'

'Wa–ah!' Poppy had woken in a bad
mood. She screamed, yelled and
wriggled, refusing to cooperate.

'Oh, not today, Poppy,' Jemma
pleaded as she filled the bath and
undressed her sister. She lowered Poppy
into the bath and splashed her with
warm water. 'I'm in a mad hurry. Be a
good girl for me.'

But Poppy stuck out her bottom lip
and looked ready to scream for
England. Jemma gritted her teeth and
prepared for battle.

Suddenly she heard a crackling sound as silver sparkles shot out of Flame's fur. His green eyes began to glow like coals and his whiskers trembled with electricity. Jemma felt a tingling sensation. She caught her breath.

What was happening?

★Chapter★
THREE

Flame raised a paw and a fountain of
silver sparks whooshed into the air.

Big, shiny, rainbow-coloured bubbles
appeared. They floated about, tinkling
like silvery bells when they bobbed
gently into each other.

'Oooh!' Poppy squealed with delight,
reaching her fat little hands up to catch
the bubbles.

'Wow!' Jemma said. 'That's brilliant.
How did you do that?'

Flame just smiled mysteriously,
showing two sharp little teeth.

Poppy gurgled happily. Each time she
grabbed a bubble it burst into a cloud
of purple, gold or silver butterflies.
They fluttered around the bathroom
before gradually fading away.

'This is great fun!' Jemma said,

giggling as a small gold butterfly landed on the end of Poppy's nose and her little sister went cross-eyed looking at it.

'What's all the laughing about? What's going on in there?' Jemma's mum called through the door.

'It's just Poppy playing with her bath toys!' Jemma called out. 'Everything's fine.'

She bit back another chuckle as Flame gently tapped a huge purple butterfly with his front paw and it turned into a shower of tiny silver sparks.

'There, finished!' Jemma said, buttoning Poppy's tiny soft shoes after they had cleared up. Downstairs, she plonked

Poppy in her playpen with some toys before going into the hall to collect her schoolbooks.

Flame followed, watching everything curiously. Just then, Jemma spotted Georgie's enormous plastic lunch box sticking up out of his school bag.

She groaned. 'Oh, no! His sandwiches! He takes mountains of them or he complains he's hungry all day at school. Mum must have forgotten. I'll have to make some now – I'm going to be so late!'

Flame's ears pricked. 'I will help!'

His fur began to sparkle again and his whiskers crackled. Jemma felt the familiar hot tingling down her spine. Flame lifted a paw and a spray of green light shot towards the lunch box.

Jemma went over and peeped
through the clear plastic lid. She saw
piles of cheese and ham sandwiches,
cakes and lemonade. 'All Georgie's
favourites! Thanks, Flame!' she said
delightedly.

'You are welcome,' mewed Flame,
looking pleased with himself.

There was a knock at the door. It
was Georgie's schoolfriends. Georgie
raced downstairs, grabbed his bag and
hurtled out of the front door. 'Bye,
Jems. Laters!' he shouted.

'Bye, Georgie!' Jemma replied with a
grin.

Mrs Watson gave her a quick hug as
she left on her way to take Poppy to
the crèche. 'Bye, Jemma. Thanks for
being such a brilliant help this

morning. Have a good day at
school.'

Jemma pulled on her school coat and
grabbed her bag. 'Bye, Flame. See you
when I get home. Be good!' she joked,
dropping a quick kiss on the kitten's
head.

Flame gave her a strange, secret smile
and began washing his ears.

★

Fran Bradshaw was waiting at the
school gate when Jemma arrived.

'Hi. Did you decide which song
you're going to do?' she asked Jemma.

'Sorry?' Jemma said, looking blank.

'Hello? The auditions for A-One Stage
School – remember?' Fran brushed a
strand of fair hair out of her eyes.

'Oh, *that* song!' Jemma remembered.
'I have a couple in mind, but I'm not
sure which I like best.' She wondered
what Fran would say if she told her
she'd been run off her feet that
morning, helped by a magic kitten!

Jemma felt the excitement rising in
her again as Fran talked about the
auditions. It surprised her how badly
she wanted to win a place at the

school. She loved being on stage.

'I was thinking about working on my routine this lunchtime. Would you mind helping me with some moves?' Fran asked.

Jemma was glad to help and anyway it would be fun. 'Sure. I'd love to. I could meet you by the playing fields,' she replied.

'OK, great!' Fran said, her blue eyes shining.

They walked into class together. Fran sat at the back and Jemma took her usual seat by the window. But as Jemma reached into her bag for her books, she gasped.

There was something warm and furry in the bag too.

Georgie! she thought. *It was one of his*

tricks. But as Jemma touched it, the furry ball began purring.

Oh, no! Flame! What was he doing here?

Jemma looked around to see if anyone was watching, and then put her face close to her bag. 'You can't come to school, Flame!' she whispered. 'We're not allowed to bring pets!'

'What is a pet?' Flame asked.

'It's . . . er, a companion animal. People own them,' Jemma hissed.

'I am not a pet!' said Flame indignantly.

Jemma frowned. 'No, you're not. But you're still not allowed to come here.'

Flame didn't seem to grasp this logic. He put his head on one side, and then his face brightened. 'I will stay. Do not worry! I will use my magic, so that only you may see me at school.'

'You mean, you can make yourself invisible just while you're here? Hey, that's cool!' She still wasn't sure about Flame being at school with her. It could lead to all kinds of problems. But it was too late to do anything about it now.

'Jemma Watson, would you like to tell us all what's so interesting about your school bag?' a sarcastic voice called out.

Mr Butler, her class teacher, had untidy brown hair. He had a way of looking over his glasses when he was annoyed.

'Er . . . Nothing, sir,' Jemma said quickly, sitting straight back up.

'Then perhaps I could have your full attention,' Mr Butler drawled.

'Yes, sir.' Jemma felt her cheeks grow hot as the rest of the class laughed.

There was a soft thump beside her as Flame jumped out of her school bag. He walked across her desk and went and sat on a window sill.

No one took any notice.

So it's true, Jemma thought. *While he's*

at school with me, only I can see him. She decided to relax and concentrate on her schoolwork.

The morning passed quickly. Now and then Jemma caught sight of Flame. Once he was sitting right beside Mr Butler, looking over the teacher's shoulder. She smiled, wondering if magic kittens could read. Later, she saw him outside chasing bees in the flower beds around the tennis courts.

At lunchtime, Jemma and Fran went out to the playing fields. It was a warm day and lots of other kids were sitting around on the grass. She could see Georgie and a group of his friends some distance away. *I bet he's enjoying his lunch*, she thought.

Fran stood up. 'I've started working on a routine. Shall I show you what I've done so far? This is the start.' She struck a pose, sidestepped, did a dip and then a twirl.

'Mmm,' Jemma said. 'It's OK, but I think you could make it more exciting.'

Fran frowned. 'I thought that too. What shall I do?'

'How about this?' Jemma demonstrated some steps. 'Now you try.'

Fran followed Jemma's moves. Both girls were in fits of giggles at Fran's first few attempts, but after a few minutes she had them off by heart. 'That's brilliant! Thanks, Jemma. It's much better now.'

'It will be better still when we do our routines to music,' Jemma said.

Fran nodded. 'I can't wait. I've been thinking about my outfit. We could go into town and buy them together. Mum says she'll take us.'

'Oh, er, right.' Jemma's heart sank. She had planned to wear something she already had. She knew her mum couldn't afford new clothes.

Just then Jemma heard shouting and whoops of laughter. She turned round and saw some kids running towards Georgie and his friends.

'What's going on?' Fran asked. 'Is it a fight?'

Jemma groaned. It looked like Georgie was up to something, as usual. 'It's my brother. I'd better find out what he's up to. Come on!' She set off at a run.

Jemma and Fran pounded across the grass. At first Jemma couldn't see Georgie for the crowd of kids round him. She pushed her way through them.

'Oh!' gasped Jemma.

Georgie stood there, a look of delighted amazement on his freckled face. He was holding his open lunch box in two hands. Shooting out of it was a multicoloured volcano of sandwiches, crisps, biscuits and cream buns!

★Chapter★
FOUR

Jemma stared in dismay at the growing mountain of sandwiches and sticky buns.

Georgie was already up to his knees in chocolate biscuits and cherry cakes. 'There's loads more. Help yourselves!' He chewed happily, cheeks bulging.

Flame's spell must be out of control. The magic lunch box showed no signs of slowing down.

'Where's it all coming from?' Fran said, frowning.

'I . . . er . . . don't know,' Jemma fibbed, playing for time.

Everyone was collecting up food and roaring with laughter. One of Georgie's friends was making a tower of jam sandwiches. Another was juggling with fairy cakes. Two more boys were skimming lemon tarts across the grass.

I have to find Flame, thought Jemma, *he's the only one who can undo the magic.*

But where was he? She spun round, slowly scanning every centimetre of the playing field. There was a tiny figure bounding about on the football pitch.

It was Flame. He was playing with two enormous pigeons.

Somehow she had to get his attention. But before she could decide what to do, she heard an angry shout. Turning round, she saw a figure striding across the playing field towards her.

'Mr Butler,' she groaned.

'What on earth is going on here?' Mr Butler's sharp eyes spotted Georgie. 'George Watson, is that you? I might have known,' he snapped, peering over his glasses.

'It's not Georgie's fault, sir!' Jemma leapt to her brother's defence.

Mr Butler rounded on her. 'Then perhaps you can tell me who *is* responsible for this mess, young lady?' he demanded.

Jemma opened her mouth to answer and then shut it again. She couldn't tell her teacher about Flame, and anyway she doubted if he would believe her.

She sent out a silent cry for help. *Oh, Flame, please come over here and undo your spell.*

'I want this stopped – now! You there, collect up those sandwiches. And you, get a bag to put those biscuits in!'

Mr Butler bawled orders to the grinning schoolkids.

'Food fight!' someone yelled. The other boys took up the chant. 'Food fight! Food fight!'

With a glint in his eye, Georgie grabbed a cherry cake and aimed it.

'Georgie! Don't you dare . . .' warned Jemma.

But it was too late. Splat! The cherry cake hit Mr Butler on the chest. Squish! A cream cake thwacked on to his glasses. The teacher's face reddened with fury and he gave a roar of rage. An enormous chocolate eclair torpedoed into his open mouth as one boy with a particularly fine aim looked very proud of himself.

Suddenly cakes, buns and sandwiches were hurtling everywhere. Jemma ducked and backed away. Georgie, his friends and Mr Butler began to disappear beneath layers of jam, sponge and cream.

Fran was trying hard not to laugh. 'I wouldn't want to be in your Georgie's shoes!' she gasped.

'He'll probably be grounded for the entire term!' Jemma said. 'Mum's going to be furious!'

Just then, she felt a small furry body rub against her leg. She glanced down with relief. 'Flame! Am I glad to see you!' she whispered.

'My magic is too strong! I will fix it,' he mewed.

As silver sparks fizzed around Flame, Jemma felt her spine tingle. Flame lifted a paw and a spray of purple glitter shot towards the food fighters. There was a puff of smoke and all the food disappeared, down to the very last ham sandwich!

For a couple of seconds no one moved.

Jemma grabbed Fran's sleeve. 'Quick! Leg it, before old Butler starts asking more questions.' Fran stumbled behind her.

As they reached the school, Jemma burst out laughing. 'I'll never forget old Butler's face when that eclair zoomed into his mouth!'

Fran stopped. She shook her head and then looked at Jemma, her face blank. 'When? What do you mean?' she asked.

'You know . . . just now . . . old Butler . . .' Jemma paused, looking puzzled. Fran obviously had no idea what she was talking about!

Other kids were sauntering back towards the school. Georgie and his friends were walking along chatting to each other. Mr Butler was striding along calmly behind them. Jemma frowned. How come everyone was suddenly acting as if nothing unusual had happened?

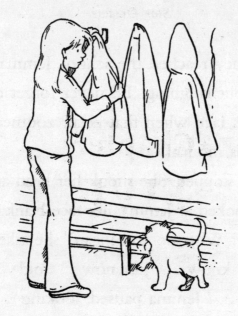

In the cloakroom, Jemma heard a
sheepish miaow at her feet. She looked
down to see Flame. 'Sorry, Jemma. I
used my magic so that no one would
remember what took place.'

Jemma laughed with relief. So that's
why everyone was acting normally.

After checking that no one was
looking, she gave Flame a quick cuddle.

★ Chapter ★
FIVE

The next day was Saturday. Fran phoned first thing.

'Can you come over to my house?' she asked Jemma. 'I'm dying to work on our routines.'

'I'd love to, but I can't right now,' Jemma said. Someone had gone sick at the supermarket and Mrs Watson had to work all day. Jemma was babysitting Poppy.

'Oh,' Fran said. 'Are you doing anything interesting?'

Jemma bit her lip. It was too embarrassing to explain that you had to look after your baby sister. 'I'm just really busy. Sorry.'

'It's OK. Maybe another time,' Fran said and rang off.

Jemma sighed. She felt awful. She could tell Fran was disappointed.

Jemma gave Poppy her breakfast, bathed her and got her dressed. 'Let's go to the park and see Georgie. He's playing football with his friends.'

Poppy gurgled happily as Jemma lifted her into her pushchair. She loved Georgie.

Flame had been stretched out on a window sill, enjoying the sun. He pricked up his ears at the promise of an outing. 'May I come too?'

Jemma patted the pushchair. 'Hop on and I'll give you a ride,' she said with a grin.

Flame jumped up and much to Poppy's delight settled himself on the folded rain hood, purring loudly. Jemma wheeled Poppy into the street and they set off for the park.

It was a hot day and there were lots
of people on the swings and boating
lake.

Jemma spotted Georgie and his
friends kicking a ball around over near
the bandstand.

Jemma parked the pushchair in the
shade beneath a tree and gave Poppy a
bottle of fruit drink. Flame shinned
up the trunk and stretched out
lazily on a branch. Jemma smiled. He
was enjoying looking down on the
world.

On the other side of the park, she
noticed some girls by the tennis courts.
They all had expensive racquets and
wore fashionable sports kit and smart
trainers.

Jemma would have loved to be able

to wear kit like that and join in with a
game. One of the smartly dressed girls
looked over and waved.

It was Fran.

Jemma waved back, her heart sinking.
She wished she wasn't wearing her
oldest T-shirt and jeans and trailing
around after her brother and sister. But
it was too late to make a getaway now.
Fran was coming over.

'Hi, Jemma!' Fran ran up beaming, her fair hair flying out behind her. 'I saw Georgie playing football with his mates and wondered if you were here. Is this your little sister?' Fran bent down in front of the pushchair. She waggled her finger so that Poppy gave her a gummy grin.

Jemma nodded. 'She's called Poppy.' She had been worried that Fran might be upset at finding her in the park after she had made an excuse not to go to her house. But she was surprised and pleased that Fran seemed fine about it.

Fran smiled. 'Isn't Poppy gorgeous? You're so lucky to have a brother and sister.'

'Do you think so?' Jemma said, surprised.

Fran nodded. 'Everyone thinks it's great to be an only child, because you get spoiled and everything. But I've always wanted a brother or sister to share things with.'

'Oh,' Jemma murmured. She had never thought of it that way. 'Well, you can share mine. Georgie's enough trouble for two families,' she joked.

Fran laughed. 'Do you have to look after Poppy and Georgie tomorrow?'

'No. Mum's at home. I could come over to your house, if that's OK,' Jemma said.

Fran's face lit up. 'Brilliant! I've been working on my song, but I need loads of practice. Well – I'd better get back to my friends now. See you tomorrow!' She reached down to kiss

Poppy's cheek. 'Bye, Poppy. Be good!'

As Fran went off to play tennis, Georgie ran over. 'I'm dying of thirst!' He grabbed a can of drink from under the pushchair. 'What did that posh girl want?'

'Don't call her that. Fran's all right,' Jemma told him.

Sunday afternoon blazed bright and clear.

Jemma and Fran were in Fran's bedroom. It was a light and spacious room with lots of posters on the walls. Jemma gently lifted Flame out of her shoulder bag, and put him on the floor.

'I thought you might like to meet my new friend,' she said.

'Oh, he's so sweet! Isn't he a lovely

colour.' Fran admired Flame's cream coat with its brown spots.

Flame gave a friendly miaow and walked over to Fran.

'He likes you. Would you like to hold him while I show you my routine?' Jemma asked.

Fran nodded eagerly. She lifted Flame into her lap and then sat cross-legged on her bed, watching as Jemma sang and danced in time to the beat.

'Da-dah!' Jemma froze in her final pose, just as the music stopped. 'How did that look?'

Fran jumped up and clapped her hands. 'That was really good!'

Flame gave a soft yowl of approval.

Fran laughed. 'Flame agrees with me!'

Jemma performed a mock bow.

'Thanks, fans,' she joked. 'All I have to do now is polish up my moves.'

'Easy-peasy. Not!' Fran pulled a face.

They heard footsteps on the stairs. Fran's mum came into the room with a tray. 'How's it going, you two? I thought you might like a drink and a snack.' She noticed Flame and gave him a friendly pat.

'Thanks, Mrs Bradshaw.' Jemma helped herself to some juice and a chocolate biscuit.

'Jemma's really good, Mum,' Fran said generously.

Jemma blushed. 'I'm not bad.'

'You'll have to get your costumes organized. Have you decided when you want to go into town?' asked Mrs Bradshaw.

'Not yet,' Jemma said quickly, feeling a bit anxious. The friendly reminder made her realize that she really must decide what to wear.

Mrs Bradshaw smiled. 'Well – just let me know.'

After a short break, Fran put her music on and she and Jemma worked on some more steps. When they were tired of practising, Fran pulled a box of

magazines from under the bed and they
stretched out together on a colourful
rug to read them.

Flame curled up with them and
began playing with a loose thread
hanging out of the rug.

Jemma was really enjoyed herself with
Fran but when she glanced at her
watch she was shocked to see how late
it was. She leapt to her feet and
grabbed her shoulder bag. 'I have to go
now! Jump in, Flame.'

Fran saw her to the front door. 'See
you tomorrow at school. Don't forget
what Mum said about our costumes.
We've got less than a week before the
auditions,' she reminded her excitedly.

'Oh, er, right.' Jemma's good mood
began to fade.

She didn't see Flame looking up at her, a thoughtful look in his green eyes.

What was the point of kidding herself, Jemma thought. She couldn't afford new clothes and there was no way she was going in for the audition in some tired old outfit. Maybe she should just tell Fran she was pulling out.

★Chapter★
SIX

'You're quiet, love,' Mrs Watson said as she wiped the kitchen table that evening. 'Is something wrong?'

Jemma sighed as she ran the iron over her school blouse. Flame was dozing on a kitchen chair beside her. 'I don't think I'll bother going in for the auditions,' she said, trying to sound as if she didn't mind.

Her mum stopped dead and looked
at her in surprise. 'But Jemma, you
were so keen! Has something
happened?'

Jemma shrugged. 'Not really. I . . .
I've just changed my mind.'

Mrs Watson frowned. She dried her
hands before coming over and putting
her arm round Jemma. 'Come on. Out
with it,' she said gently.

Jemma's worries started to spill out
and once she started she couldn't stop.
'It's just that I haven't got anything to
wear. Fran's going to get a new
costume, and I bet everyone else will
too, except me! I'm going to really
stand out and look stupid in front of all
my friends!' She hung her head. 'I
didn't want to tell you, Mum. I know
we can't afford to buy anything new.
Anyway, it doesn't matter now. I've
made up my mind. I'm not going in
for the auditions.'

'Hmm.' Mrs Watson looked
thoughtful. She opened a kitchen
cupboard and took out a tin. 'Would
this help to change your mind?' she
said, pressing some money into Jemma's
hand.

'But that's for your winter coat. You've been saving for it for ages!' Jemma looked at her mum in amazement.

'I've still got lots of time to save up again. You need a costume and we're going to get you one,' Mrs Watson said firmly.

Jemma gave her mum a huge hug. 'You're the best mum in the world!'

Flame sat up suddenly and began purring loudly. He gave Jemma and her mum a wide, catty grin.

'I know it sounds strange, but I reckon that kitten understands every word we say,' Mrs Watson said with a chuckle.

Jemma smiled to herself, but said nothing.

★

'Be careful you don't fall!' Jemma said to Flame as she walked down the street swinging her school bag on Wednesday.

'I am fine, thank you, Jemma,' mewed Flame happily as he tiptoed across the tops of fences and garden gates, keeping pace with Jemma.

His ears were pricked and his tail stuck up jauntily. The sunlight made the brown spots on his cream fur really stand out.

'I can't wait until I see Fran,' Jemma said to him. 'We can arrange to go into town and buy our outfits together now!'

Flame purred in agreement. He batted at a bumblebee and almost lost his balance.

Jemma chuckled and reached out to

steady him. Just then, someone came barging round the corner and knocked right into her.

Jemma stumbled and almost fell over. 'Hey!' she called angrily at the back of the stocky figure that carried on walking right past her.

'What?' He turned round and came back. Jemma recognized him now. It was Sam Thomas, a tough boy from their school who picked on some of the younger children – even Georgie sometimes.

'Uh-oh,' she murmured.

'Well, if it isn't that freckly kid's sister,' Sam scoffed. 'Is that your kitten? What a fleabag!'

Before Jemma realized what was happening, Sam reached out and grabbed Flame by the scruff of his neck. As the boy pulled him off the fence, Flame mewed with alarm. His body just hung there and his legs and tail dangled down.

He was helpless.

'Stop it! Put him down!' Jemma fumed.

'Let's see if he can fly!' Sam pretended to throw Flame over a nearby garden wall.

Flame gave a terrified wail. His paws scrabbled at thin air. He seemed too scared to do any magic. Or maybe he didn't want to give himself away.

Jemma's stomach clenched. 'Please don't hurt him!' she begged.

Sam lifted his hand slowly, higher and higher, ready to fling Flame into the air.

He's really going to do it, Jemma thought. She felt desperate. She had to help Flame. But what could she do?

'Wait!' she cried. Plunging her hand into her pocket, she took out her outfit money and showed it to Sam. 'Let him go and I'll give you this.'

Sam's eyes lit up greedily. He reached for the money.

Jemma snatched back her hand. 'Give me Flame first,' she demanded. Her knees were shaking, but she made herself stare boldly at the mean older boy.

Sam made up his mind. 'Here. Have your stupid kitten.'

He thrust Flame at Jemma and grabbed the money. Without a backward glance, he went on his way.

Jemma's hands trembled as she cuddled Flame. The thought of him being hurt gave her a horrible sick feeling. 'I've got you. You're safe now,' she said softly.

Flame dug in with his claws and clung tightly to her school jumper. He looked up at her with round, troubled eyes.

'Jemma, all your money has gone,' he whimpered.

'It doesn't matter,' she told him, rubbing her chin on his soft head.

She tucked Flame into her school bag, where he curled up next to her pencil case. She kept her hand in her bag, stroking him gently until he began to purr.

Jemma grew calmer as she walked to

school, but her spirits were low.

There was no way she could tell her
mum that the money had been stolen.
And her last chance of buying an outfit
for the audition was gone for good.

The school day seemed to pass by in
a blur. Jemma's class were doing
medieval history, but Jemma just
couldn't concentrate. How was she
going to enter the audition without
an outfit?

At least Flame seemed no worse
after his ordeal. Jemma had to smile.
She watched Flame jumping round
the classroom from desk to desk. He
seemed very interested in the open
medieval history books. Once, she saw
him staring at a computer screen,

dabbing at the keyboard with his paw.

Jemma hurried home when school finished. It was her mum's late night at the supermarket. She planned to get tea ready for when she came home.

Just as she let herself into the house, she heard a crash.

'Oh, heck!' shouted a voice.

'Georgie! Is that you?' Jemma called. He was supposed to be playing with a friend after school.

Georgie stuck his head round the kitchen door. There was flour all over his face and his hair stuck up in white powdery spikes. 'Hi, Jems!' he said brightly. 'I came straight home. I've got a surprise. I'm making tea!'

Jemma had a strange sinking feeling.

She slowly pushed open the kitchen
door.

Mounds of flour covered the table
and the floor. White footprints trailed
all through the house. Sticky red
fingerprints smeared the wall, the fridge
and the cooker.

'Jam tarts!' said Georgie proudly.

Jemma was speechless.

Mum was going to go mad!

'In the shower – now!' she ordered Georgie.

He scowled but did as she told him.

She dashed towards a cupboard and took out the vacuum cleaner. Plugging it in, Jemma switched it on. There was a loud bang and a puff of black smoke.

The vacuum cleaner had died.

'Oh, that's just great!' Jemma burst out. She felt like dissolving into tears. She'd had a horrible day and it wasn't getting any better.

There was a shower of sparks as Flame jumped on to the kitchen table. 'I will help,' he mewed.

Jemma felt the warm, magical tingling and wondered what was going to happen next.

A moment later, the vacuum cleaner

burst into action. It zoomed about madly, making clean trails through the flour. 'Must clean up! Must clean up!' it hummed, trundling into the sitting room.

'Wow! Thanks, Flame,' Jemma said. She grabbed a cloth and began scrubbing at a sticky, jammy fingerprint. Her mum would be home soon. With a bit of luck, she might have time to clear up this mess.

Just then she heard the vacuum cleaner give a loud cough and then it burped.

Jemma stood in the doorway, staring in horror at the scene before her. The vacuum cleaner wove back and forth, sucking up everything in its path. It swallowed a pile of books and a

jumper, and began chomping the
curtains.

'Oh, heck!' Jemma gasped. It looked
like the cleaner was going to gobble up
the whole room!

There was a faint sound above the
din. Jemma's head came up. It was the
front door closing.

Mum was home!

★Chapter★
SEVEN

'Flame! Do something!' Jemma wailed.

Flame's whiskers crackled as he lifted
a paw. A comet's tail of gold sparks
flew all round the room.

Bang! The vacuum cleaner whizzed
back into the cupboard. Swish!
Cushions, carpets and curtains flicked
back into place. Phloop! Flour and jam
disappeared back into bags and jars.

Mrs Watson came into the kitchen, carrying Poppy.

'Hi, Mum,' Jemma said breathlessly. 'Did you have a good day?'

'Not bad,' her mum said, smiling. 'My goodness! You and Georgie have been busy. Everything's sparkling clean. And what's that cooking?' She opened the oven door. 'Jam tarts. Lovely.'

Jemma grinned at her mum. 'Georgie made the tarts. With a bit of help!' *And a great big dollop of magic*, she thought.

Jemma went straight up to her bedroom after tea, before her mum started asking questions about when she was going to buy her outfit. She wanted to put off telling her about

the money for as long as she
could.

Flame followed her into the room.
He rubbed himself against her legs. 'Do
you need an outfit?' he mewed.

Jemma nodded sadly. 'Yes, I do. But
it's not going to happen, is it?'

Flame put his head on one side. His
tail stuck up jauntily. A couple of sparks
flicked out of the end. 'Close your
eyes!' he miaowed eagerly.

Despite herself, Jemma smiled. What
was he up to? She closed her eyes. A
familiar tingling spread all over her.

'Look now!' Flame told her.

Slowly, Jemma opened her eyes. Her
jaw dropped as she stared at her
reflection. 'Oh, my goodness,' she
gasped.

She wore a long dress of yellow silk
and bright-red velvet. It had a V-neck
and trailing sleeves. On her head there
was a tall, pointed hat with a floaty
veil.

Flame had made her a medieval
costume! Jemma's heart sank. Flame
must have got the idea from one of
her classmate's textbooks at school
that day.

'Do you like it?' Flame asked proudly, his tail in the air.

'It's . . . er . . . beautiful,' she stammered. 'But I can't wear it for the audition. How would I dance in it?'

Flame looked dejected. 'Is the dress wrong, Jemma?'

'No, not at all,' Jemma said quickly, not wanting Flame to feel bad. She bent down to stroke him. 'I love it. Really, I do. I'll keep it for a fancy-dress party,' she promised. 'Thanks, Flame.'

'You are welcome!' Flame cheered up.

He gave her a whiskery grin. Jumping back on to the bed, he began licking his fur.

'Jemma! Could you come down here,

please?' her mum called up the stairs.

'Coming, Mum!' Jemma quickly took
off the dress and put it in her
wardrobe.

She found her mum in the hall,
filling a bag with books. 'I've just
remembered these library books.
They're due back today. Be a love and
take them for me, will you? The
library's open until seven p.m.'

'OK.' Jemma checked the time. It was
already 6 p.m. 'I'll go now.'

It took only a few minutes to walk
to the library. She handed the books in
and still had time to look around.

In the children's section, there was a
rack of magazines. Jemma chose one
and spread it open on a table. It had
pictures of pop stars, a problem page

and loads of stuff about make-up and hairstyles.

As she flipped a page, she saw a photo of a girl in a red T-shirt decorated with bright ribbons, buttons and sequins. It looked really expensive and it was just the type of thing Jemma would have loved to have worn.

As Jemma closed the magazine, a brilliant idea jumped into her head. That was it! Her problem was solved. But would Fran agree with her?

Jemma phoned Fran the moment she got home. She told her about the photo of the gorgeous T-shirt. 'Why don't we make our own outfits? It can't be that hard. We've already got jeans and T-shirts. And my mum's brilliant at sewing. I could ask her to help us!'

'And no one else would have anything like them!' Fran got caught up in the excitement. 'My mum's got a big box of sewing stuff. It's got ribbons and sequins and loads of other things in it. I'll ask her if we can use some of that.'

'Great!' Jemma said, then she bit her lip. 'I've just thought. It's Thursday tomorrow. The auditions are on Saturday!'

There was a short silence before Fran replied. 'We can do this! But we'll have to work on them Thursday and Friday night. How about if I come to your house straight after school?'

Jemma hesitated. She still felt doubtful about letting Fran see her messy house. Then she remembered how friendly and relaxed Fran had been with Poppy.

'OK. I'll tell my mum,' she decided. 'I'm sure she won't mind. But we'll have to think of something to keep Georgie out of the way!'

Fran chuckled. 'Leave it to me!'

With Fran coming round, Jemma decided she was going to have to tell her mum what happened to the costume money.

She went into the sitting room where Mrs Watson was on the sofa reading the local newspaper. Jemma sat down next to her. 'Mum, I've got something to . . .' she stopped in surprise as she spotted a familiar name in the paper. 'That's Sam Thomas, from my school! Why's he in the paper?'

'Apparently an old couple caught him pinching apples from their back garden,' her mum told her. 'The old lady chased Sam with her walking stick and he fell backwards into their garden pond. Her husband took a photo as Sam tried to climb out. Do you know this boy?'

Jemma nodded. 'Sam Thomas is really mean. A lot of kids are scared of him.'

She told her mum about bumping into the older boy on the way to school. 'Sam threatened to throw Flame over a garden wall. I thought he was going to do it. So I gave him the money for my outfit to stop him. I'm really sorry for losing the money, Mum, but I didn't know what else to do.'

There was a long pause and then Mrs Watson sighed. 'I'd probably have done the same thing in your shoes.' She slipped her arm round her daughter's shoulders. 'I bet you've been worrying yourself sick about this, haven't you? You should have come and told me straight away.'

'I know,' Jemma said, feeling better for having got it off her chest. 'Next time I will!'

'Good.' Suddenly Mrs Watson began
chuckling. 'Look at this! I'd say that
bully got what he deserved, wouldn't
you? This will be all round your school
tomorrow!'

She opened out the newspaper so
that Jemma could see the picture of
Sam Thomas crawling out of the
muddy pond with waterweed piled on
his head and dripping from his ears.

The old lady stood there, waving her stick at him.

'He doesn't look so tough now, does he?' Jemma fell about laughing as she imagined all the schoolkids seeing the picture of the mean boy.

Sam Thomas would never live it down.

On Thursday, Fran's mum gave Jemma and Fran a lift home. 'Don't forget this! And these.' She passed Fran the big box full of sewing stuff and a pile of football magazines. 'Have fun, girls. I'll pick you up later, Fran. Bye!' She drove away.

Georgie's eyes lit up when he saw the magazines. 'I borrowed them from our next-door neighbour,' Fran explained with a grin.

Jemma chuckled. They would keep him quiet for hours. Now they could get on with sewing without Georgie 'helping'.

It was Mrs Watson's half-day. She had supper ready. Afterwards, Jemma and Fran cleared a space on the kitchen table and spread out their T-shirts.

Fran sorted through her mum's old sewing stuff. 'Wow! Look at this sparkly braid. I love these pink sequins.'

Jemma chose some colourful ribbons and glittery purple beads. As Jemma and Fran set to work, helped by Jemma's mum, Flame wandered into the kitchen. He mewed a greeting.

'Hello again, Flame,' Fran said.

'Did you have a nice sleep?' Jemma

got up and tipped some dry cat food into a bowl.

Flame crunched it up, purring loudly.

'Isn't he cute? Like a ball of brown and cream fluff with big green eyes!' Fran admired Flame. 'When did you get him?'

'He hasn't lived here for long. But it feels like I've always had him,' Jemma said fondly. It was difficult to even imagine life without Flame now.

A few hours later, the T-shirts were looking good but there was still loads of work to do. And they hadn't even started on their jeans.

'Fran's mum will be here soon,' Mrs Watson said. 'I think it's time you stopped for now. Tell me what you want doing and I'll carry on for a while.'

'Thanks, Mum,' Jemma said gratefully. Her fingers were starting to ache with all the hand sewing.

Fran's mum arrived and Jemma waved to her friend as the car pulled away. There was just time to practise her routine before she went to bed.

The next day at school, she and Fran grabbed every spare moment to practise their songs and moves. They did their routines in the corridor between lessons and even ate lunch while dancing and singing.

'Maybe I should add this move to my routine!' Fran joked, posing with a sausage roll in one hand and a carton of orange in the other.

'Definitely! It's a real winner!' Jemma said, giggling.

Straight after school they went back to Jemma's house and began sewing.

'Your mum's brilliant!' Fran held up her jeans. The pockets and hems glittered with braid and sequins.

'Yes, she is,' Jemma agreed. Her jeans had seams decorated with silver and purple beads. Mrs Watson had even made a matching belt of plaited ribbons.

By the time Fran had to go, their outfits were finished. Jemma hoped she'd never set eyes on another needle and thread! But she had to admit, the outfits looked fantastic.

'Tomorrow's the big day!' Jemma said to Flame as he snuggled up beside her on the bed.

She was sure she wouldn't sleep a wink. But she fell asleep the moment her head hit the pillow.

On Saturday morning, Jemma could hardly concentrate on helping her mum deliver papers. She felt nervous but excited. In just a few hours she would be performing her routine in front of a panel of judges.

Back at home, Mrs Watson made a quick sandwich but Jemma was too nervous to eat anything.

'Sit here, love, so I can do your hair,' her mum said. She brushed, pinned and sprayed Jemma's long brown hair and then carefully applied some stage make-up.

Jemma peered at herself in a mirror. 'It looks great, Mum. Thanks!'

She went upstairs to her bedroom, folded her outfit carefully and put it in a shoulder bag. Flame was stretched out on the window sill, sunning himself.

'It's time to go and meet Fran at the town hall,' Jemma said to him.

'Shall I come too?' he mewed, jumping down.

Jemma gave him a quick cuddle. 'Of course you can. But you mustn't do any magic. I have to do this all by myself. Deal?'

Flame nodded seriously.

Mrs Watson came out to give her a hug and wish her good luck.

'Thanks, Mum. See you later,' Jemma said.

As she set off down the street, she began to sing her song to herself. But after the first line, she stopped. She couldn't seem to remember any of the words. Maybe they'd come to her if she concentrated on her routine. But it was no use. The whole thing seemed jumbled up in her mind.

A horrid, uncomfortable feeling crept up on Jemma. Her stomach churned and her knees began shaking. The thought of facing the panel of judges filled her with sudden panic.

'It's no use, Flame. I thought I could do this, but I can't!' she burst out.

Flame looked up at her and whimpered softly.

Jemma stopped, trying to decide what to do. She couldn't bear to go home and face her mum's disappointment, but there was no way she could face Fran either.

Crossing the street, she started walking quickly, with no idea of where she was going.

Flame padded along beside her in silence as they wove through the streets, then as they turned a corner he suddenly bounded ahead.

'Jemma, come!' Flame instructed as he purposefully made his way across the road and through some tall, decorative iron gates.

Jemma looked up in surprise. They were at the park. She hadn't realized how far she had walked. But where was Flame going? He had never taken off like that before.

She quickly checked the road for cars and then dashed into the park after him.

'Flame! Where are you?' she cried urgently as she jogged across the grass and checked out the flower beds. Then she caught a glimpse of cream and brown fur over by the bandstand, but by the time she got there he had gone again.

When she finally caught up with him by a park bench, she was out of breath. 'There you are, Flame! Why did you run off?' she panted, flopping down on to the seat.

'You told me that I was not to do

magic,' Flame told her, leaping up to crouch beside her. 'But I had to help you somehow.'

As Jemma stroked the top of Flame's fluffy head, she realized that her attack of nerves had faded. Running after Flame had made her forget all about herself, which was just what he'd planned! She felt much better now. Just to test herself, she went through the song in her mind. She could remember every single word.

'Will you go to the audition now?' Flame purred hopefully.

'I don't know . . .' Jemma took a deep breath. She thought of Fran waiting there for her and made up her mind. 'All right. Let's go!' she said, jumping to her feet. But a quick glance at her watch filled her with dismay. 'Oh, no! I'm so late. I'll never get to the town hall in time. Unless . . .' She looked down at Flame. 'I know I said you mustn't use magic to help me win, but can you help me get there, please?'

Flame grinned as his fur began glowing with sparks and his whiskers crackled with electricity.

★Chapter★
EIGHT

Jemma felt a bump as she landed. She was in a cubicle in a ladies' toilet — wearing her new outfit! She could hear lots of nervous voices talking about the auditions. She was inside the town hall.

Opening the door, she poked her head outside. There was a long queue of people twisting all down the corridor. Just then Fran came out of a room, looking hot and breathless.

She rushed straight over. 'Jemma! Where have you been? I thought you weren't coming. Quick, it's your turn next. They're waiting for you.'

There was no time to explain anything. Fran opened the door and almost pushed Jemma inside.

Jemma's heart pounded as she saw the judges sitting at a long table. She introduced herself and gave them her music tape.

'All right, Jemma. Show us what you can do,' one of the judges said with a smile.

Jemma took up her starting position.

This was it! All her hard work had brought her here. Her hopes and dreams of going to stage school were pinned on the next few minutes.

As the music filled the room, Jemma began her routine. As she sang and danced, she forgot to be nervous. The sheer joy of performing carried her along. She twisted, jumped and swayed in time to the beat.

It was going fantastically well until she missed a step and almost slipped over. But in a split second she had covered the mistake and carried on smoothly. She gave a final flourish and finished. Breathing hard, she straightened up.

She searched the judges' faces but couldn't tell what they were thinking.

'Thank you, Jemma. You'll hear from us in a few days.' The judges smiled coolly.

She recovered her tape, thanked the judges politely and went outside.

Fran was waiting for her. 'Well? How did it go?' she asked at once.

Jemma's shoulders sagged. 'OK at first, but I made a stupid mistake. I don't think they were very impressed.

They didn't say a word about how I did. How about you?'

'The same,' Fran said, pulling a face. 'But they told us earlier they haven't time to discuss the routines. There's too many people to see.'

'Really?' Jemma said. Maybe she was still in with a chance.

But she couldn't convince herself. That mistake had been stupid and clumsy.

Maybe she had been fooling herself to think she could win a place at stage school anyway.

'How about a barbecue in the garden?' Mrs Watson suggested the following evening.

'Good idea.' Jemma tried to sound

enthusiastic. She knew her mum was trying to cheer her up. 'Come on, Flame. Let's go and tidy the garden.'

Mrs Watson laughed. 'I hope that kitten can use a lawnmower!'

Jemma hid a smile as Flame padded into the garden after her. If only her mum knew!

There were some boxes of flowers outside the back door. Her mum had got them cheap when the supermarket had a clear-out, but hadn't had time to plant them.

'Maybe I spoke too soon,' Jemma sighed as she looked at the tangle of weeds, long grass and scruffy paving stones. But Flame took one look at it and sparks leapt out of his fur. There was a silver flash! Jemma screwed her eyes up against the light. When she was sure it was OK again, Jemma slowly opened one eye, holding her breath in anticipation.

The garden was transformed!

The flowers were all planted and the lawn had been mown. The paving stones were weeded and swept.

'It's perfect. Mum's going to love it!' she scooped Flame up and buried her face in his soft fur. 'Thanks, Flame! I'll tell her I had a lot of help from a friend with the gardening. It's true in a way, isn't it?'

Suddenly Flame stiffened. She felt him begin to tremble.

Jemma frowned. 'What's wrong?'

'I sense my enemies close by!' he mewed nervously. 'I must go soon! I need to find a new hiding place!'

Jemma felt her stomach clench. She had known this moment would come eventually, but she had never wanted it to. What would she do without Flame? Jemma looked at the trembling kitten and sighed. She knew she was going to have to be stronger than this. Flame was in danger. If his uncle's spies found him, he would be killed. 'You should go, now!' she forced herself to say.

Flame shook his head. 'I must build up my magic. It takes time.'

'You'll be safer in the house.' Jemma took him in and ran up the stairs two at a time. 'Maybe you could hide inside my wardrobe?'

She made a nest out of some clothes. Flame crept right inside and curled up. His big green eyes and pink nose were all that could be seen. He looked very tiny and vulnerable.

Jemma felt scared for him. A wave of heavy sadness washed over her. First, she had almost certainly lost her chance to go to stage school. Now she was going to lose Flame. She didn't think she could bear it.

'Jems! Mum's got the stuff for the barbecue.' Georgie came to fetch her.

'She says I can cook the sausages, if
you help me.'

'All right, I'm coming.' Jemma made
a huge effort to push her worries aside.
She definitely wasn't hungry any more.
She took a last look at the wardrobe
where Flame was hiding and then
slowly followed Georgie downstairs.

Jemma didn't sleep well that night. She
had nightmares about fierce cats chasing
Flame and woke when it was still dark.

Flame had crept in beside her. She
cuddled up to him, feeling dreadful. His
little furry body was comforting.

'I wish you could stay here forever,'
she murmured.

'I cannot,' Flame mewed sadly. 'In my
homeland I will be king, one day.'

Jemma nodded sadly. 'I know.'

The next time Jemma woke it was time to get up. She was pulling her school jumper on when she heard the sound of the letter box. The post was here!

When she came into the kitchen, her mum held out an envelope. It was the results from the audition. Any minute now she would know the bad news.

Jemma felt sick. 'Will you read it, please, Mum?'

Mrs Watson opened the letter slowly. As she read, her face changed. 'You've done it, Jemma! You've won a scholarship!'

Jemma's jaw dropped. She couldn't believe it. 'Let me see!' She scanned the letter with shining eyes. 'They think I'm talented. And they were impressed because I didn't let a small mistake put me off . . .' She looked up. 'Oh, Mum. I've done it! I'm going to stage school!'

Mrs Watson gave her a big hug. 'I knew you'd do it! I'm so proud of you, love!'

Jemma had to tell Flame. She almost flew up the stairs.

'Flame, I'm going to stage school!'

she cried, pushing open the door. 'I did it, all by myself. And . . . oh!'

There was a bright silver flash. On the rug stood the elegant white lion. Silver sparks glittered in his fur like a thousand fireflies.

Prince Flame! He was no longer in disguise as a cream and brown kitten. Jemma gasped. She had almost forgotten how stunning he was in his true form.

An older-looking grey lion stood next to Prince Flame. 'We must hurry, Your Highness,' he growled urgently.

'You're leaving right now?' Jemma asked, her voice breaking.

Prince Flame's emerald eyes crinkled as he smiled sadly. 'I must. My enemies come ever closer.'

Tears came to her eyes. She managed a shaky smile. 'We had a great time, didn't we? I'll never forget you.'

She stretched out her hand. Prince Flame lowered his head and allowed her to stroke him one last time before he backed away.

'Be well. Be strong, Jemma.' He raised a shining white paw in farewell.

Both cats began to fade. There was a final spurt of silver sparks and they were gone.

Jemma wiped her eyes. Something glittered on her bed. It was a single silver sparkle. Reaching out, she picked it up. It tingled against her palm before blinking out.

'Be safe, wherever you go, Prince Flame,' she murmured.

Just then she heard a knock on the front door. An excited voice called through the letter box. 'It's me, Fran! My letter came this morning. I've got some brilliant news!'

Jemma took a deep breath as she thought about Flame for a moment longer, then she hurtled downstairs, a huge grin breaking out on her face.

'So have I!' she shouted.

10 things you should know about Flame

1. Whatever kitten colour he takes, Flame's eyes are always bright emerald green. He is very unusual because when he is in his true form his fur is completely white.

2. Flame is a loyal friend and never forgets those who are kind to him.

3. Flame tries hard to get things right, but he sometimes makes mistakes . . . which can lead to funny results!

4. Flame is tiny in his kitten disguise, but he is always brave and steadfast. He has a big heart and is very curious about everything.

5. Of course, Flame's even more than a super-duper magic kitten. What is he? Here's a clue – ROAR!!

6. Flame is very affectionate and has a super-loud purr, but he chooses who can hear it – just like he chooses who is able to see him.

7. Flame loves being in our world, having adventures with different people, and learning new and exciting things.

8. Flame is not keen on bullies, whether they're mean kids or animals. He's likely to let them know it, too!

9. Flame loves to help people with their problems, but not always in ways they expect!

10. Flame often appears suddenly and without warning. Look out for him. He might come to visit you next!

Spot the Difference

There are six differences between pictures A and B from **Star Dreams**.
Can you spot them all?

Answers on the last page.

Odd One Out

All these pictures of Georgie from
Star Dreams are exactly the same – except one.
Which one is different from the others, and why?

Answer on the last page.

Magic Kitten

Double Trouble

Kim discovers how to cope with
her mean cousin when a fluffy silver
tabby kitten comes to stay . . .

SUE BENTLEY

Magic Kitten
Double Trouble

A sweet silver tabby kitten needs a friend!

puffin.co.uk

Answers

Spot the Difference

Odd One Out

Picture E is different – the shirt pocket is missing.

For lots more Magic Kitten fun, visit

www.puffin.co.uk/suebentley